PENELOPE'S PROTEST

Douglas Hill was born and raised in western Canada. After graduating in English, he moved to London (where he still lives) in 1959 and worked in publishing before becoming a full-time writer.

He has written more than fifty books for adults and children including non-fiction works and a number of science-fiction anthologies.

Penelope's Protest is the second adventure story featuring Penelope and her magical pendant.

Also by Douglas Hill in Piper

Penelope's Pendant

PENELOPE'S PROTEST

Douglas Hill

Illustrated by Annabel Spenceley

PIPER
PAN MACMILLAN
CHILDREN'S BOOKS

First published 1994 by Pan Macmillan Children's Books
a division of Pan Macmillan Publishers Limited
Cavaye Place London SW10 9PG
and Basingstoke

Associated companies throughout the world

ISBN 0 330 32727 5

Text copyright © 1994 Douglas Hill
Illustration copyright © 1994 Annabel Spenceley

1 3 5 7 9 8 6 4 2

A CIP catalogue record for this book is available from
the British Library

Phototypeset by Intype, London
Printed by Cox & Wyman Ltd, Reading, Berkshire

FOR ROSEMARY

who has her own magic

CHAPTER 1

A Glint in the Eye

For Penny and her family, it was an ordinary evening in early autumn. Yet it was also the start of something that would quickly become extra-ordinary, as well as amazing and sometimes even terrifying.

They had been watching television, which was reporting on a robbery in town that day. Two masked robbers had held up a jewellery shop and stolen a lot of diamonds, worth millions. Penny's father muttered something about crime getting worse everywhere, her mother shook her head sadly, and her older brother Alan wondered if the robbers would get away with it.

Then, during a commercial break, Penny's mother made a small, ordinary announcement.

"I'll be home late tomorrow evening," she said, "so you'll have to make supper for yourselves. I'm taking the Green group to hand out leaflets about what's happening to Cheppingstone Woods."

No one was surprised. Penny's mother was an energetic and capable woman who was involved with many good causes, on top of having a job and looking after her family. The environment was one of the causes closest to her heart, and she was secretary of the local Green group.

So, at her announcement, the others just looked resigned. Penny's father sighed and might have said something, but Alan got in first.

"*Bo*-ring," Alan said. He was a thin, spotty four-teen-year-old whose normal way of speaking was mostly jeering and mocking. "All the lettuces, out annoying people."

Lettuces – "greens" – was what Alan usually called his mother's Green group, and anyone else who was concerned about the environment. Sometimes he changed it to "spinach" or "cabbages". The joke hadn't been very funny, Penny thought, the *first* time he had said it.

"Can we get pizza tomorrow?" Penny asked hopefully.

Then she saw the glint in her mother's eye and went silent. Her mother was small and pretty and usually quite nice – but when she got *that* look in her eye, anyone with any sense kept quiet.

"I thought perhaps my family might come and

help with the leaflets," Penny's mother said through her teeth. "But I see that's too much to ask. You're too selfish and lazy, like most people, to do anything to help protect the environment."

"Bo-ring," Alan murmured – very, very quietly.

"Just what's being done to the Cheppingstone Woods?" Penny's father asked, trying to change the subject a little.

"The local council," Penny's mother replied, her eyes still glinting, "has sold a huge piece of the woods, just off the highway, to some businessman named Roche, who is going to build an industrial estate – factories and warehouses and paved roads, all kinds of mess and pollution . . ."

"Could mean a lot of jobs," Penny's father said mildly.

"Certainly," her mother said. "But there are plenty of other places that could be built on. Such as that disused railway yard on the edge of town. But, no – this Roche and the council have to go and ruin one of the most unspoiled beauty spots in the whole area!"

That was true enough, Penny thought. She and her family had often driven out for picnics in the Cheppingstone Woods, which were many broad acres of healthy woodland full of splendid old trees, low grassy hills, secluded dales full of flowers in summer ... It was horrible, Penny thought, to imagine all that beauty being spoiled by huge ugly factories with smoking chimneys and trucks everywhere.

"So," her mother was continuing, "we're having a protest in front of the town hall, handing out leaflets and asking people to sign a petition. Tomorrow, when people are on their way home from work."

Alan snickered. "You and your lettuces", he said mockingly, "ought to try and catch those two robbers who stole the diamonds. Then you'd be heroes, and everybody would listen to you."

As the look in her mother's eye grew more steely, Penny sat back with a smile. Alan never seemed to know when to keep quiet, and now he was in trouble. For a moment Penny felt almost tempted to go with her mother to hand out leaflets. Because she did feel upset about what was to happen to the woods – and because, if she sided with her mother, it would annoy Alan. Which was always enjoyable.

But perhaps not, she thought, if it meant giving up pizza for supper.

Later that evening, Penny was upstairs in her bedroom, supposedly getting ready for bed. She was kneeling by her dresser, reaching in to the back of the bottom drawer, bringing out a round disc of metal with a chain, like a pendant.

It was not much to look at. Just dullish silvery metal, thinner at the edge than in the middle, with several scratches and some deep dents. Oddly, though, its thin metal chain seemed to *grow* out of the disc without any sort of attachment that could be seen. For anyone looking closely, that was the only outward clue to how unusual the pendant really was.

In fact, it was a *magic* pendant.

Penny had found it at the seaside, in the early summer, and had soon learned to her astonishment and delight that magic didn't happen only in stories but really existed.

The pendant's magic, though, was a special sort. It *moved* things, and did nothing else. Penny could use it to fetch things or send things away, to lift things or lower things, to throw things around. She could also use it to move herself, even flying herself into the air like a feather on the breeze.

At least, she could if she dared. But there was danger in using the pendant, as Penny had also learned.

The pendant had been damaged, a long time before. The deep dents in it had once held jewels, which had contained some part of the magic. But since the jewels had been lost, the magic no longer worked properly. Nor could it ever be fixed.

When Penny had first used the pendant's magic, she had soon learned that it almost always went wrong, somehow. The results might be no more than messy, which could be simply annoying or amusing or both. But just as easily, the use of the magic could be highly risky. Back in the summer, when Penny had used the pendant to get out of trouble, the magic had gone so wrong that it had put her into even *worse* trouble, and quite a lot of danger.

After that, Penny had put the pendant away in the bottom drawer and hadn't brought it out even to look at more than once or twice. But on that autumn night she brought it out again, putting the chain around her neck and looking at herself in the mirror.

In the glass she saw a slim eleven-year-old girl of average height, heart-shaped face, brown hair and brown eyes, in her own opinion quite ordinary and maybe even plain. Just as anyone glancing at the pendant would have thought it a very plain sort of ornament. But Penny, knowing better, smiled at herself in the mirror.

My magic, she thought, and her smile became a

sigh. If only it worked properly. For a moment she thought of what she might do with magic that really worked. She would go out with the pendant and right wrongs, she thought. She would save the Cheppingstone Woods, somehow. And she would catch the two robbers who had stolen the diamonds. And she would . . .

She sighed again. And then it occurred to her, in a little teasing edge of an idea, what if by some magical accident the pendant had started working properly, while it lay in her drawer? She knew in her heart that the idea was silly, but she couldn't resist the hope.

So – for the first time since she had put herself into danger in the summer – she called on the pendant's magic.

She took it into her hand, though she didn't need to since she was wearing it. Then, in her mind, she simply *asked* it to do what she wanted. At once, as the magic acted, she felt the pendant's metal grow warm, as it always did.

She hadn't asked much of it. She had merely sent the magic across the room to turn down her bed. The task couldn't have been simpler. Yet it went wrong.

The unseen power of the pendant jerked the bed-clothes completely off the bed. It jerked them with

such force that it pulled the mattress aside as well, so that it fell against the bedside table, which toppled over with a crash. And the bedclothes flew across the room and dropped in a clinging heap on top of Penny, so that she too fell over with a crash.

"Pen-*el*-ope!" That was her mother, calling from downstairs in *that* tone of voice. "Are you in bed yet?"

Penny fought her way free of the bedclothes. "Almost!" she called. Then she got up and angrily began to put her room back together.

Luckily her lamp had not broken when the table fell over. And soon she had dragged the mattress back on the bed and spread the covers back over it. Then she turned the covers down by hand, took the pendant off and looked at it with another sigh.

There was no other sound in the room as she did so, yet something made her lift her head to look at the shadowy far corner of the room.

She jumped, and gasped, as if with shock.

Someone was standing in that corner. Someone wearing a long hooded cloak. Someone whose face was mostly in darkness, so that all Penny could see was a long nose – and large ears that came to sharp points at the top.

CHAPTER 2

Out of Reach

As the weird cloaked figure moved towards Penny, she relaxed and smiled. "Hello, Glumdole," she said. "You made me jump."

The cloaked figure, moving into the light, was revealed as a strange little man in an old-fashioned tunic and high boots under the cloak. His skin was greyish and hairless, his face was lined and droopy, his eyes were sorrowful, his whole expression looked miserable.

"Hello, Penelope," he said. He didn't return her smile, but his small mouth looked as if it didn't know how. "I didn't mean to startle you. But it's been a long while since I felt the pendant's magic – so I thought I'd come and see what you were up to."

Penny nodded, without surprise. She knew that Glumdole could sense the magic of the pendant, over some distance. That was because Glumdole was the one who had made the pendant in the first place.

Glumdole was a *cobold* – one of what he called the Magic Folk, along with gnomes and elves and all the rest. And he was sad and gloomy by nature, Penny had learned, probably because there was hardly anyone around any more who knew about cobolds or believed in magic or did anything the way it had been done in Olden Times.

When Penny had first found the pendant, Glumdole had magically come into her room at night looking for it – and terrifying her in the process. But they had become friends, and Glumdole had told her all about the pendant and how it had been damaged.

He also told Penny that the pendant should be destroyed, because it could be dangerous. But, he said, the pendant was Penny's, because she had found it, and no one could *force* her to have it destroyed. So she hadn't. Although after her first adventures with it had ended in near-disaster – when Glumdole had had to rescue her – she had taken his advice and had put it safely away.

"I took the pendant out to look at it," Penny explained, "and I just thought I'd try it, once again." She shrugged. "It still doesn't work."

Glumdole nodded gloomily. "No. It won't, you

11

see. Not properly. Not ever." He paused, gazing sadly at the pendant in Penny's hand. "Still, it's nice to see you. You haven't called me in a long while."

Penny felt a little guilty. When they had first become friends, Glumdole told her that they then had a "name-tie". That meant that if she wanted or needed Glumdole, she merely had to speak his name and he would magically appear. It was the name-tie that had brought Glumdole to her aid when she was in danger. But afterwards, she had felt that it would be wrong to bring Glumdole to her whenever she felt like it. It was too much like someone calling a servant, or a parent calling a child.

"I've thought of calling you," she said. "But then I always think you might be busy or something. So . . . I don't."

Glumdole nodded sadly. "That's kind of you, Penelope. I do often have things to do. And I've been meaning to call you, before now. To invite you to visit me. For tea, perhaps."

Penny looked interested. She had never been to Glumdole's home, and wasn't sure exactly where it was. "I'd like to," she said at once.

"Ah. Good." Glumdole looked even more sorrowful. "But now I won't be able to do so for a while. I have to go away. On a visit – to see an aged cousin of mine, who needs my help."

"Is your cousin in trouble?" Penny asked.

"Not entirely," Glumdole said. "He lives in some mountains a long way from here, in a place where humans have started building all sorts of things. As humans do – ruining all the peace and quiet. He has asked me to help him look for a new home."

"That's too bad," Penny said. "How long will you be gone?"

"I have no idea," Glumdole said. "But I promise to come and see you as soon as I return. And then you must come for tea."

"Fine," Penny said. "I hope you find a good place for your cousin. It's a shame that he has to move." She frowned slightly. "You're right about people ruining nice peaceful places. It's happening around here, too."

Quickly she told him about the horrible things that were going to be done to the Cheppingstone Woods, and how her mother's Green group were the only ones trying to stop it.

"I wish I had magic that *worked* properly, like yours, Glumdole," she said. "Then I'd do something about it!"

Glumdole peered at her worriedly. "No, no, Penelope," he said. "If you were one of the Magic Folk, you'd know that we *never* meddle that way in the business of humans. The way the world is

13

now, it could be dangerous if we caused people to start believing in magic again."

"Why?" Penny asked. "I don't understand."

Glumdole sighed. "No. Well. You see, this world has been made the way it is now by *science* and all that. Bring magic back into it, and everything could start coming apart." He saw Penny's puzzled frown and sighed again. "Well. Never mind. I'll explain it another time, when you're older. Now I must say goodbye for a while, and let you get to bed."

"You *will* be back, won't you?" Penny asked.

"Yes, yes," Glumdole assured her. Then he frowned. "I hope you'll be careful with the pendant while I'm away, Penelope. Try not to *do* anything about your woods or anything else."

"All right," Penny said with a shrug. "Why not?"

"Because I will be a long way away," Glumdole told her. "And the magic of our name-tie is limited. It can reach only over *short* distances." He peered at her, still frowning. "This is very important, Penelope. If you speak my name while I'm with my cousin, I won't hear it. If you get into trouble again, with the pendant, I won't be able to come to your aid."

After that warning, Glumdole said goodbye and vanished, as he always did, with a twitch of one pointed ear. And Penny tucked the pendant back in the bottom drawer and finished getting ready for bed.

But later, as she drifted off to sleep, she thought drowsily to herself that what Glumdole said, about not meddling, wasn't fair. What was the point of having magic power – even a damaged sort – if you couldn't use it to make things better?

She was still thinking along those lines the next evening, when her mother came home and made another announcement.

While the Green group had been handing out leaflets by the town hall, that afternoon, they had seen a big display set up by the council, about how wonderful all the factories and things would be when they were built in the Cheppingstone Woods. The Green group then had the idea of setting up their *own* display, with photographs and charts and drawings, showing how much damage would be done to the woods.

"So this Sunday", Penny's mother announced, "the group is going out to the woods to take pictures and do some measuring. I think some work has already been done on the site, so there may already be some damage to be shown."

"All the cabbages going to the woods!" Alan jeered. "Be careful the rabbits don't eat you!"

"*And*," Penny's mother went on, giving Alan one

15

of her steely looks, "I thought it would be nice if we *all* went. We could take a picnic."

Penny's father looked dismayed. "Oh . . . uh . . . I don't think . . ." he mumbled. "I've got so much to do in the garden . . ."

Alan was also upset. "*I* can't go," he said. "I'm . . . uh . . . going out with my friends . . . they're all expecting me . . ."

Penny watched the glint gathering in her mother's eyes. And though Penny didn't really think it would be much fun to spend a day with the Greens, she had no plans of her own for Sunday. And she saw a very good way of annoying Alan and getting one up on him.

"I'll go," she said brightly.

"*Thank* you, Penny," her mother said firmly. "I'm glad that *someone* else in this family can spare an unselfish thought for the environment."

She stalked off to the kitchen. And as their father hid himself behind his newspaper, Alan gave Penny a baleful glare.

"I hope you and all the cabbage-heads have a *rotten* time!" he said sourly, and stamped out of the room.

Penny smiled. Whatever happened in the woods on Sunday, she thought, she'd tell Alan that it had been great fun, the best time ever. That would annoy him even more.

16

And, she thought, she would wear the pendant on Sunday. Despite what Glumdole said about not meddling. Of course, she'd be careful with it, she promised herself. But she'd wear it. Because there was no way of knowing *what* might happen, on the day.

CHAPTER 3

Voices from the Ground

Sunday, when it arrived, was a perfect early autumn day. A cloudless blue sky, warm sunshine, the air clean and fresh with a fragrant tinge of smoke from bonfires of dry leaves. Penny thought that the Cheppingstone Woods was *exactly* the place to be on such a day, and said so cheerfully at breakfast – aiming to make her father and brother feel uncomfortable, and succeeding.

The drive out to the woods was very peaceful, which made Penny glad that Alan hadn't come. Her mother even let her listen to whatever music she liked, on the car radio. But she had to put up with an interruption while her mother listened to the news. It seemed mostly concerned with the continuing search for the two men who had stolen the diamonds. The police had found their getaway car, on the edge of town – but the robbers were thought to have left the area.

"I wish our Green group would get as much attention from the news people as those robbers," Penny's mother said. "*Then* we'd save the woods."

Penny smiled as she imagined her mother and the Green group robbing a bank to get some attention. And she smiled at the thought again when they reached the woods and found the group waiting.

There were only ten of them – twelve counting Penny and her mother – and they were of course ordinary, law-abiding people. There were a few more women than men, more older people than younger, all dressed for a day in the country. They were also all cheerful, kind-hearted, concerned people who seemed delighted to see Penny. And she found it hard not to giggle at the idea of them all becoming desperate criminals to get noticed by local radio.

So she was a bit shocked, a while later, to find that the Green group wasn't entirely law-abiding, after all.

They walked into the woods from the road, enjoying the fresh air, the sunshine, the autumn colours of the leaves, all the beauty around them. The group seemed excited to be out *doing* something, with cameras and notebooks, planning their big display. And then they arrived at the site where the factories and everything were to be built.

"It's the nicest bit of the whole woods!" Penny said.

And the others, looking sad or angry or both, agreed that it probably was.

The site was a broad, low area – like a very large basin. On its sides the land sloped up to form low hills and ridges that made the raised edges of the basin. Trees of all sorts grew thickly all over the basin and up the slopes of the hills, along with dense thickets of bushes. But there were partly clear areas as well, where some late-blooming flowers showed their colours amid the rich grass.

"In the spring," Penny's mother said to her softly, "this vale and the hillsides are *full* of wildflowers, just dazzling."

One of the older men pointed. "They've started work," he said sourly.

Penny saw that some trees and bushes had been cleared away, here and there across the basin. The bare patches of earth, looking like wounds, held a great many lines of wooden stakes.

"That's the surveying," the older man went on. "Just waiting for the bulldozers, now."

"Not if we can help it," Penny's mother said firmly.

They all set off down the slope, looking more

grim and serious now, in the face of the task that awaited them. Then they halted again, seeing something that made them look even grimmer.

At the foot of the slope, like a line drawn through the woods, a number of signs had been nailed to trees. Signs that said PRIVATE PROPERTY and KEEP OUT, and others that said NO TRESPASSING and TRESPASSERS WILL BE PROSECUTED.

"What's prosecuted?" Penny asked.

"Being arrested and taken to court," her mother said calmly.

"*Could* they prosecute us just for walking around here?" asked one of the younger men.

"Certainly," Penny's mother said. "The council sold the land to that businessman, Roche. It's private land now."

"And Roche would love to prosecute us," someone said. "We're a nuisance to him, and he'd be glad of a way to get rid of us."

The group stared at the signs in silence – then all of them turned to Penny's mother, as if to be told what to do.

She shrugged. "We can't let a few signs stop us now," she said. "As long as there's no one around to see us, let's go ahead. It's not as if we're going to do any *damage*. Let's just do what we've come for, as quickly as we can."

21

Looking pleased, the group strode boldly forward past the signs. And while Penny was feeling a bit shocked at their readiness to break the law, or anyway bend it a little, her mother smiled at her.

"I hope you won't tell anyone about this," she said. "If we got into trouble over it, it could be serious."

"I won't say a thing," Penny promised – imagining the remarks that Alan would make if she and her mother were arrested for trespassing.

The Green group then spread out across the basin, taking photographs, sketching, measuring, scribbling notes. And Penny, wandering around, began to have the oddest feeling – that they were being *watched*. Some of the others also seemed to feel eyes upon them, and kept looking nervously around at the trees and bushes.

But there was no one to be seen, anywhere, and no one rushed out to drag them off and "prosecute" them. So everyone relaxed, after a while, and got on with their work. All except Penny.

She was the only one there with nothing to do. She had no camera, and didn't know what sort of pictures were needed anyway. So she just wandered, idly, still wondering about that weird feeling of being watched. And at last she drifted away towards the trees.

Her mother saw her, but let her go after Penny

had promised not to go too far or stay away too long. Then, carefully and watchfully, Penny slipped away through the trees that led to the west side of the basin.

She was planning to make a big circle, around the edge of the basin, staying up on the hillsides as she went. If she went quietly enough, she thought, she might just see if anyone *was* hiding somewhere, spying on the Green group, causing that spooky feeling.

When she reached the hillside where she would start her circle, she was feeling pleased with herself. In her opinion, the world's most brilliant and skilled woodsman – or woods*woman* – could not have moved through those trees more stealthily than she had. Hardly a leaf had rustled or a twig snapped. And she hadn't had the feeling of being watched for some while. Except by one squirrel and several birds.

On she went with her circle around the basin. It was fun, creeping along the wooded hillsides, pretending to be a wilderness heroine from an adventure story. But then she came to one particular hillside that was not only quite high and steeply sloping, but was also completely open and treeless, covered only with the thick grass or turf and a few low, ragged bushes.

If anyone else was creeping around in those

woods, nearby, she would be exposed. But still she wanted to go on – so she started across the steep grassy slope at a half-run. Halfway across, she saw a sudden movement on the edge of her vision and stopped, her heart beating fast.

But then she relaxed, smiling. It had been a lolloping leap by a big grey rabbit, fearfully vanishing over the sharp ridge at the top of the slope.

Out of interest, Penny trotted up to the ridge-top to see if she could see the rabbit again. It was of course out of sight, but she did find a number of holes in the ground, higher on the slope, that were surely burrows, or had once been.

She peered into a few, knowing she wouldn't see anything. Then she moved away, no longer running, no longer worried about being seen. In truth she was getting a little bored with her wilderness-hero game, and was wondering if she'd bother going on with the circle around the basin. And then she halted, seeing that the choice had been made for her.

Her way was barred, by a large gap in the ridge where she was walking. It was a deep cleft, like a small ravine – as if a giant knife or saw had carved an immense notch out of the ridge. The cleft had very steep sides, nearly straight up and down like cliffs. And it seemed to be choked with a dense and tangled growth of brush.

That does it, Penny thought. To continue her circle, she would have to go all the way down the steep slope where she was standing, get past the mouth of the ravine and then climb back up the next hillside beyond the ravine. She didn't really think it was worthwhile. Instead, she thought, she'd just go down the slope and wander back to the site to see if her mother and the Green group were finished yet.

But she took only one step before she stopped, going motionless, as if she had suddenly become a statue.

Behind her, at the top of the ridge, she heard men's voices.

Slowly she turned to look. Again she went statue-still, eyes wide.

There was no one there. She saw nothing but empty grass and a few rabbit-holes.

Then she jumped, as the voices spoke again. They seemed to come out of the air, fairly loud but muffled in an odd way. And with the voices came a smell. Tobacco smoke, just a hint of it, wafting in the air.

Half-crouching, Penny crept nervously up towards the ridge-top. There she noticed quite a large rabbit-hole that she hadn't seen before. But, looking at it closely, she saw that it was peculiar.

The opening of the hole was a very neat circle. And there were stones placed all around the opening, as if to protect the edges.

People made that, she told herself. And she crept up to that unnatural hole, wanting to look down it, to see what could be seen.

But she stopped, frozen as before, when the voices started up again. Definitely coming from that hole in the ground. Along with more wafts of tobacco smoke. And, weirdly, with the faint burble of running water, sounding hollow and distant.

Being closer, Penny could hear the voices more clearly. They were the voices of two men, it seemed. Rough, ugly voices that sent a shiver along Penny's spine.

But she felt an even colder shiver when she heard the word that told her what the voices were talking about.

They were talking about diamonds.

CHAPTER 4

Robbers' Cave

The two robbers, Penny thought, stunned. They're *here*. Somehow they're inside the hill . . .

Warily she peered down into the hole where the voices were coming from. She saw nothing but blackness, as if there was a bend in the hole. But the voices were clearer – and sounding like the two were arguing.

"I still say we're all right here!" one man said, his voice sharp and rasping. "If we just sit tight . . ."

"Sit tight," the other repeated, his voice thick and sullen. "We got no *choice* but to sit tight. We might've been miles away – but you said no, you said we should leave the car an' hide out a while . . . An' now we're stuck here, an' the place is full of people! All those workmen, the last few days, an' now those weirdies out there. . ."

Crouched silently on the ridge-top, Penny nodded. He means the Green group, she thought.

So we *were* being watched, when we first got here – by these two.

"Come on, Frank," the first voice said. "This ain't a bad place to hide. It's even got runnin' water and a hole for a chimney in the ceiling. People've lived here before, I reckon."

"Sure," growled the second one, Frank. "Tramps an' such. An' cave men, prob'ly."

"We're better off here, all the same," the first one insisted, "than if we tried to move the diamonds, with every cop in the area lookin' for us. 'Specially now they got our car."

The one called Frank grunted. "Yeah – an' *you* said the car'd be all right, Ed."

"So the cops got lucky," snarled the first one, Ed. "An' if we leave here an' go wanderin' around out in the open, they're likely to get lucky again. They'll still be watchin' trains and buses, an' everythin'."

"Maybe," Frank said sullenly. "But what if some of those weirdies come lookin' around here? An' what about when work starts over on that site? It's gonna be *crawlin'* with people around here when that happens."

There was a long pause, as if for thought. "You got a point there, Frank," Ed said at last. "But maybe work won't start for a while. Maybe every-

29

thin' will cool down enough for us to get goin' before it starts."

"An' maybe it won't," Frank grumbled. "We don't *know*, do we?"

"We might find out," Ed said thoughtfully. "We might just go an' ask the weirdies. I bet they'd know."

"Go *out*?" Frank sounded horrified. "When we're supposed to be hidin'?"

"We'll say we're a couple of hikers, just passin'. Nature-lovers." Ed laughed harshly. "They won't suspect a thing."

"They better not," Frank growled. His voice seemed to be farther away, as if he and the other man were moving.

Then Penny heard a muffled sound of metal grinding on metal. Flattening herself into the grass, she wriggled carefully forward and peered down over the edge of the ravine.

Amid the dense brush, below her, she caught sight of the two men moving away from the side of the cliff. As they pushed their way through the thickets, with much rustling and crackling, Penny began to creep down the slope. Shortly she saw the men again, just two dark figures striding away through the trees, heading towards the Green group. She then hurried down the rest of the way, until she was standing in front of the mouth of the ravine.

It was not an appealing sight. At ground level it was hard to see that there *was* a ravine, because of the tangled jungle of brush and trees that filled it. And many of the bushes were thorny, making the barrier worse. It was a good hideout, Penny thought. Not many people would want to fight through those thorny thickets just to see what might be in the ravine.

But Penny wanted to. So she took a deep breath, glanced around to be sure she was alone, and went in.

Spotting a few places where branches had been pushed aside by the robbers, she followed their vague trail. It was hard and painful going. Thorns stabbed her and sharp twigs jabbed her – scratching her skin, pulling her hair, snagging her clothes. But she persisted, until she came at last to the robbers' hideout.

A cave, in the wall of the ravine.

The opening was no more than a narrow slit in the earth and stone of the ravine, about twice Penny's height. And it was blocked off. A barrier of corrugated iron nailed on to heavy planks was firmly wedged into the opening. So, she thought, the grinding of metal that she had heard, from above, would have been when the robbers moved the barrier so they could come out, then replaced it again.

She guessed that the cave-opening had been blocked up to prevent accidents. Especially to keep children out, she thought, since the tall barrier would be too heavy to be moved by a child.

At least, she thought with a smile, an *ordinary* child.

And then she sent the magic of the pendant reaching out.

She felt the pendant grow slightly warm, as she asked it to move the barrier – and to move it carefully, only a little way. The pendant may have tried, but its damaged magic had no delicate controls.

Nothing much happened except that one small corner of the corrugated iron bent slowly back, as someone might fold over the corner of a page.

Penny frowned. "Come on," she whispered to the pendant, "*move* the thing!"

Growing warmer, the pendant obeyed. The barrier swung sharply out from the cave-mouth, as if it was on hinges. It swung all the way around – to slam against the side of the ravine with a clanging crash and a burst of earth and dust.

Penny went into a frozen crouch, heart hammering, as that crash echoed through the woods. But no one came plunging through the thickets to investigate the noise. As the echoes died away, stillness and soft birdsong returned to the woodland.

At last Penny stood up, peered around once more at the greenery, took another deep shaky breath, and went into the cave.

It was a fairly narrow little cave, with a high ceiling. And she saw with relief that a few posts and beams had been put up to support the ceiling. The wood of the supports looked old and a bit rotten, but they were better than nothing. She also saw the robbers' scattered belongings – two narrow camp beds with dirty sleeping bags, two knapsacks with clothes spilling out, a box of tinned and packaged food, a small lamp, a camp stove. The floor of the cave was littered with old newspapers, empty cans, cigarette butts and other rubbish.

There was no sign of anything that looked like diamonds.

Still, in the light from the cave's opening, and a little that gleamed faintly from the hole in the ceiling where she had heard the voices, she searched. Under the sleeping bags, among the litter . . . In her search she found that a small, rapid stream of water was pouring into the cave at the back, forming a good-sized pool. She remembered hearing water, from above, and she paused by the pool, studying it thoughtfully.

The stream of water entered the cave through a

long crack in the earthen wall, poured into a large natural pit like a kind of bowl to make the pool, then seemed somehow to drain away. Maybe it goes underground, Penny thought, remembering something about underground rivers from school.

The pool itself didn't look deep, but it was hard to be sure in the dimmer light at the back of the cave. On impulse, she dipped her hand in. The water was quite cold – and the pool did turn out to be shallow. Because her fingers touched something lying on the bottom.

Something that felt like a plastic bag. A bag that was folded over and sealed into a small parcel – which seemed to be full of hard, sharp-edged things like stones.

Or diamonds.

Penny jerked the plastic bundle out of the water, stared at it wildly for a second, then leaped for the cave-mouth with the bundle clutched in both hands. With the robbers' loot there in her hands she was suddenly near to panic, terrified that they might come back at any second and catch her.

She burst out of the cave and plunged away through the brush-filled ravine, ignoring the jabbing, grabbing thorns. In a few moments she was rushing breathlessly up the grassy slope again, above the cave. And there she flung herself full-length on the soft turf, gasping for breath, hardly able to believe that she had actually gone into the lair of the villains, stolen their loot and got safely away.

Sitting up, she sucked at a thorn-scratch on her hand, then studied the plastic bundle. The bag had been folded over tightly and sealed with heavy-duty plastic tape. It looked like being hard to open without strong scissors or a knife. Anyway, she thought, she probably shouldn't open it. It should stay as it was until she handed it over . . .

Then a terrible thought struck her. *Could* she hand it over? To the police or anyone?

If she did, everyone would want to know how she had got it.

She could just hear the questions. How had she managed to move the heavy barrier, by herself, from the cave-mouth? And what were she and her mother and everyone doing there anyway, on a site marked PRIVATE PROPERTY and TRESPASSERS WILL BE PROSECUTED?

For some moments she sat there on the hillside and tried to find answers. But it was no use. She couldn't tell anyone about the pendant, and she couldn't get the Green group and her mother into trouble.

At last, with a sigh, she moved along the slope to one of the rabbit burrows that she had found before. It looked like it hadn't been used by rabbits for a long time, so she stooped and shoved the plastic bundle into the hole. Then she stamped on it with her heel to wedge it in more deeply, and finally scattered dry leaves and dead grass over it until it was hidden.

When she was done, she started down the slope. And then she nearly jumped into the air as the silence was shattered by a terrible cry, behind her.

The sound came from the larger hole in the ground that she had found before – the cave's airvent or chimney. And it was a cry made by two voices together, almost a howl, full of shock and savage fury.

The robbers were back in their cave, and had discovered their loss.

The awareness of danger sent Penny into a frantic dash down the slope. But when she reached level ground, and began to rush away through the trees, she slowed for an instant and glanced back.

Fear struck her like a club, turning her icy-cold again, holding her still. Through the trees she could see the thickets at the mouth of the ravine. And out of those thickets she saw two men emerge, crashing wildly into the open. Both were in dark clothing, one tall and one short.

And as she saw them, they saw her. For the tall one gripped his companion's arm, and pointed directly at her.

CHAPTER 5

Anxious Days

That sight sent Penny dashing away through the trees as fast as the undergrowth and lashing branches would allow. To her relief, no one came after her, and in a few moments she found her mother and the Green group, just finishing up their work.

"I was just going to call you," her mother said, smiling. Then the smile faded as she looked at Penny more closely. "What have you been doing to yourself? Look at your clothes – and those scratches! And you're all flushed..."

"I was running," Penny said quickly. "And I – I got stuck in some thorn bushes."

Her mother sighed. "More mending."

But she wasn't really upset. She seemed quite cheerful, Penny thought, probably because the day had gone well. And on the way home her mother chatted merrily about what they had done, the good pictures they had taken, the ideas they had worked out for the big display that would show everyone how the woods would be ruined.

"Just remember not to talk about our trespassing," she told Penny seriously. "Not to anyone. The council would be glad to have a reason to get the Green group into trouble."

"I won't say anything," Penny promised. I *can't* say anything, she thought to herself gloomily. That's the problem.

"I must say," her mother went on with a laugh, "those two young men who came along gave us a fright. At first we thought they were guards or something. Did you see them? They were very nice – just out walking, they said, though they didn't look all that outdoorsy. They seemed really interested in our protest, and in what was happening on the site."

I can imagine, Penny thought, with cold shivers flickering along her spine. And for the rest of the drive home she remained silent, anxiously pondering her problem.

By the next afternoon, after school, she thought she had an answer. She would simply phone the police and tell them about the robbers and the diamonds, without saying who she was or anything. It seemed like a good idea. But it didn't work.

The policeman on the other end of the telephone guessed at once that she was a child, and wouldn't even listen to her. He just kept demanding her name and address – and when she didn't give them, he told her angrily to stop wasting his time with stupid games, and hung up.

So she went back to her anxious pondering. She thought of calling Glumdole for advice, then remembered that he was away, out of reach of their name-tie. She was all alone with her problem – and her fears.

She was mainly afraid that the robbers, having seen her in the woods, might be searching for her, to get their diamonds back. That thought made her nervous, at first, whenever she left the house. But soon she began to feel that she was being afraid for no reason.

After all, she thought, the robbers would surely have expected her to report them. They wouldn't know she had good reasons not to. So they might already have fled, thinking that the police would come after them.

Also, it occurred to her, even if the robbers had seen her they might not think that *she* had the dia- monds. They would never guess that she could have moved the heavy barrier from the cave-mouth.

And since the robbers had *already* been worried

about work starting on the site in the woods, as she had overheard, there was a good chance – she told herself – that they might have left for that reason, too. At the least, they'd be likely to leave when work *did* start.

So, as the days passed and her fear faded a little, she began to have another idea. When the work started in the woods, she would try to go to the area somehow and get the diamonds out of the rabbit-hole. Then she would simply *leave* them at the main police station, without saying anything, trying not to be noticed.

It wasn't exactly a great plan. But it was the best she could do.

During those days of Penny's pondering and worrying, her mother and the Green group had been very busy. They had set up their big display, and they spent a lot of time with it. It was set up in front of the town hall, and when Penny went to see it she found that it was attracting a lot of attention. She stayed awhile to help, handing out leaflets to people who wanted to know more, which pleased her mother very much.

She was also pleased to find Penny being deeply interested in all the news broadcasts, on radio and television. "I'm so glad to see you getting concerned about the world's problems," her mother said to her.

In fact, Penny was mostly concerned with her own problem – hoping that some broadcast, some day, would say that the robbers had been caught. But it didn't happen. And, as the days went by, Penny found that she had got herself into another problem, as well.

Her mother by then thought of her as a fully-fledged member of the Green group. (Alan had started calling her different "green" names, including broccoli-brain, but that didn't matter.) So Penny had to trail along with her mother to all the Green group's meetings, and try not to yawn too openly during all their talk.

And she felt it would be just more of the same when one evening her mother made another announcement.

"The council is taking our protest seriously," she told her family, at the supper table. "The Mayor has invited the Green group, and any interested members of the public, to a big meeting on Saturday. There's a report about it in the paper today. The council will probably try to convince everyone that what's happening to the Cheppingstone Woods will be a perfectly good thing."

"When on Saturday?" Penny's father asked.

"In the afternoon," her mother replied. "In the town hall. There'll be refreshments and everything. Sparing no expense to try to shut us up." She glanced around the table. "I don't suppose you'd like to be there . . . ?"

As before, Penny's father looked dismayed. "Not me. There's the garden . . . a *huge* lot of things to do, this time of year. I was really hoping that you might be able to come and help me . . ."

Penny's mother waved her hand in the direction of Alan, who was hunched over his plate shovelling food into his mouth. "Alan can help you . . ." she began.

"*Me*?" Alan sat up, looking outraged. "I've got things to *do* on Saturday."

"You can help your father," Penny's mother said firmly. "It won't take all day."

Alan began a prolonged moan about how he had to do everything and it wasn't fair and why couldn't Penny do it, until his mother stopped him.

"Penny," she said pointedly, "will want to be at that meeting as much as I do."

Penny wasn't at all sure about that. But when Alan glared at her, muttering "broccoli-brain", she quickly nodded. "It'll be fun," she said, smiling sweetly at Alan, which made his glare more furious.

And, she thought, she might learn at the meeting when the construction work was going to start, in the woods – which she was sure would drive the robbers away if they hadn't already gone.

If nothing else, she thought, there *will* be refreshments at the meeting.

Time plodded on, bringing no better ideas to Penny about solving her problem. And, in time, Saturday arrived, when Penny and her mother and the Green group went to the meeting in the town hall. And because of her worries, because for some reason she felt better that way, Penny made sure to wear the pendant, hidden as usual under her shirt.

The meeting was to be in a committee room in the town hall. It was a long, bright room with a high ceiling, two gleaming chandeliers and a pair of glass doors at the far end leading on to an ornamental balcony. Several rows of chairs had been set out in front of a table where, Penny's mother said, the Mayor and others would sit.

But Penny was more interested in the two longer tables at either side of the room. One of them held a marvellous model of the factories and things to be built in the woods, with perfect little buildings, tiny model trees and bushes. The other long table, covered with a white tablecloth, held a great many plates heaped with things to eat, along with bottles of soft drinks and a tall silvery urn of coffee.

Penny wanted to look at those tables more closely, but her mother stopped her. "You can look around later," she said. "After the speeches and everything."

Sighing, Penny stayed where she was, looking around at all the pictures on the walls and on special stands – photographs, blueprints and artistic drawings, showing the site in the woods as it was and as it would be. She also gazed for a moment through the double glass doors, but there was only sky to look at, with a few clouds being whipped along by an autumn wind. So, instead, she watched all the other people. Many were still coming in, making quite a sizeable crowd. And then, with a jolt of excitement, she saw one group carrying equipment that included a television camera.

Wouldn't Alan be jealous if I got on TV, she thought happily, and watched with keen interest as the television people got set up for filming.

"Didn't I say our protest is being taken seriously?" her mother said to her. "The local newspaper and radio are here too. We can *really* make our views known!"

She turned away, calling a greeting to someone,

and Penny went on watching as the crowd gathered. Some important-looking men had come in by then, taking seats at the table in front of the rows of chairs, holding papers that were probably their speeches. Let them be *short* speeches, Penny said to herself.

Beside her, she heard her mother's voice, mentioning her name.

"Yes, this is my daughter, Penelope," her mother was saying. "She was out at the site, last Sunday. Did you see her?"

Penny turned, to see who she was talking to. And she went absolutely still, her insides feeling as if they had turned to frozen slush.

The two men with her mother were youngish, wearing leather jackets and jeans. One was tall and bony, the other was short and burly. Both looked fairly unremarkable. But to Penny they were terrifying.

She had seen them before – in the Cheppingstone Woods.

The robbers. Just a few paces away from her. And glowering at her, with rage and a dire threat showing in their eyes.

47

CHAPTER 6

Typhoon

"Penny, this is Ed and Frank," her mother said brightly. "We met them in the woods last Sunday, and they've come to support us today. Isn't that nice?"

"Yeah, we read about this do in the paper," the tall one said to Penny's mother, in the sharp rasping voice that belonged to the one named Ed. "Thought we'd come along."

To look for me, Penny thought.

"Right," said the short one, who would be Frank, with the thick, sullen voice. "Thought we'd see what's what."

They were still glaring at Penny as they spoke, but her mother didn't notice. "It's very good of you," she said. "We need as many people as we can get."

"Any idea yet", asked the one called Ed, "when they're startin' work out there on the site?"

Penny's mother shook her head. "We haven't

heard. They may tell us here, today. There'll be a chance to ask questions after the speeches."

"Good," Ed said, still eyeing Penny. "We'd like to get some questions answered."

Penny wanted to turn and run. But it was time for everyone to take their seats, to get things started – and as Ed and Frank moved away to find chairs for themselves, Penny relaxed a little. They can't do anything to me *here*, she thought as she sat down beside her mother. Not with all these people.

So she settled back as a man in a blue suit stood up at the table in front of the audience and began speaking. He was the town Mayor, Penny understood – and she didn't like him a bit. He was pretending to be all jolly and friendly, but his smile was false, his warmth and sincerity were false. Like people trying to sell you things in TV commercials, Penny thought. Even his *hair* looked false, she thought with an inward smile. A wig of some sort, not quite fitting, not quite the right colour.

The Mayor was also having a bad time with his speech, for the autumn wind outside was growing stronger. It was loudly rattling the double glass doors, each gust drowning some of the Mayor's words. His smile was beginning to slip as he went red in the face, but he went on for a while, before introducing another speaker.

This one was a tubby man with grey hair and

a grey suit, who turned out to be Mr Roche, the businessman behind all the development in the Cheppingstone Woods. He went on for quite some time as well, without saying much. And then it was time for questions.

Penny paid attention again when her mother rose to ask why the factories couldn't be built on a certain disused railway yard on the edge of town. And Roche replied in a very superior manner.

"Our experts studied both sites," Roche said loftily, "and in the end rejected the railway yard. For reasons that are probably too technical for housewives."

Penny saw anger flare in her mother's eyes. "You mean it's *cheaper* to ruin a beauty spot!" her mother said heatedly.

But Roche was turning away dismissively, while the Mayor was looking elsewhere. "Let's let others ask some questions," the Mayor said in his falsely warm voice.

"I will *not* be patronized," Penny's mother hissed furiously, as one of the Green group ladies patted her arm sympathetically. Penny wasn't sure what patronized meant, but she felt sympathetic too. After that the questions trailed away, as everyone realized that Roche and the Mayor were there only to put *their* arguments, not to listen to others. So it was time for the refreshments, and the people got up and milled around, looking vaguely disappointed but also vaguely hungry.

Penny's mother stormed away to try to confront the men who had dismissed her so rudely. Leaving Penny, for the moment, alone. And she turned to see the two robbers bearing down upon her.

She tried to slip away, but people were blocking her path. Trying to dodge past a cluster of chatting adults, she found herself trapped against the wall near the door. And there Ed and Frank caught up with her, looming in front of her, glaring.

"We want to talk to you," Frank growled.

"We think you know where somethin' is that belongs to us," Ed snarled.

"An' I'd like to know how you got *into* the cave," Frank said.

Ed shook his head, scowling. "Never mind that now. Just tell us where the . . . where they are."

Penny stared up at them, shivering. All around her were friendly adults, yet none of them had noticed her plight. She thought of yelling for help – but she couldn't. The two men weren't really *doing* anything to her. And she wouldn't be able to explain how she knew what they were.

"Come on," Ed snarled. "Talk. Or . . ."

But his words were drowned by an echoing

rattle, as another strong gust of wind shook the double glass doors. Someone yelped in surprise at the noise, and the two robbers looked around to see what was going on.

Penny saw her chance. Perhaps, at the back of her mind, she also saw a way to strike back. Not just at the robbers, but at Roche and the Mayor, the organizers of the meeting, who had been rude to her mother.

She hurled the power of the pendant at the glass doors – and at the wind, outside.

As the pendant grew hot, the glass doors came open. But more than that. They flew violently apart, opening inwards and smashing against the walls, glass shattering, wood splintering, half-torn from the hinges.

And what came storming in through that opening was no longer just a strong autumn wind. Swollen by the wild power of the pendant, it had become a mighty gale, nearly a typhoon.

Inside the room, it became a disaster.

At the gale's howling impact, everyone in the room reeled and staggered, crying out with shock. The two robbers had to clutch at each other to keep their balance. And Penny ducked away, out into the room.

It was almost impossible to stay upright, as the ferocious wind lashed her. Crouching low, she struggled across the room towards the refreshment table, where she had last seen her mother. Around her the adults were fighting their own battles against the wind, their cries mingling wih the wind's shriek as they stumbled to and fro, tripping over the chairs that were being flung like matchwood across the floor.

Glancing back, Penny saw with some relief that the robbers were not after her. Most of the people were trying to get to the door, in a wavering, lurching stampede – and the robbers were caught up in that. So Penny struggled on. While the typhoon destroyed the room.

In the first moment of its entry, the wind had ripped the pictures and blueprints from their fastenings. They were now torn to bits, being whirled around in the air like the fragments of ruined kites. Some of the tiny buildings and trees from the model of the construction had also been snatched up by the gale, to be flung here and there like miniature missiles.

Then, as Penny glanced around, she saw one of the chandeliers – which were twisting and swinging crazily in the gale – tear loose from its fastenings. It fell in a frightening explosion of glass, directly on to the table holding what was left of the model.

The gale screamed as if in triumph and swept that table clear, glass and bits of wood spraying over the floor. By then the typhoon had also collected the papers brought in by the officials – all their tedious speeches – flinging them into the air to join the shredded pictures. The storm of flying paper in the room became an almost blinding blizzard.

But Penny was drawing near to her goal, the refreshment table, though she could no longer see her mother in the storm of flying objects and the surging crowd. She cried out, but her voice was lost in the howl of the wind and the wailing of the people – who were not managing to get out of the room. The door opened inward, and with too many panicky people pressed against it, plus the force of the wind, it seemed impossible to open.

Then, as if to add insult to injury, the typhoon found new missiles. Its raging strength snatched up objects from the top of the refreshment table, and hurled them around. Paper cups and plates were added to the blizzard of flying paper – and so too was the *food*.

Biscuits and canapés, soggy halves of sandwiches and sticky slices of cake flew through the air. At once most people in the room were wearing fragments of cheese and tomato and tuna and ham,

splatters of buttery bread, smears of icing and cream, like weird decorations on their clothes and skin.

And despite her fright and her struggle, Penny laughed aloud as a particularly thick cream cake soared past her and struck the Mayor neatly between the eyes.

The Mayor had been tottering towards the door, holding his wig on with one hand, clutching at Mr Roche for support with the other hand. As the sticky cake struck him, he cried out and began to wipe the smeared cream from his eyes – with the hand that had been holding his wig. The wind gleefully snatched the hair-piece away.

With shiny bald head and cream-smeared face, the Mayor squealed in anguish and went in pursuit, dragging Roche with him. The wind whooped down on them, its strength throwing them backwards. Together they stumbled against the refreshment table, jostling into the tall, unsteady urn that held the coffee.

The spout of the urn, like a vindictive mouth, spat a thick hot stream of coffee all down the fronts of both men's suits.

They squealed together at that, and staggered away, moaning. In the same moment a flying chocolate eclair struck Penny squashily in the middle of her shirt, and stuck there for an instant. At once she grabbed it, glanced around again, saw that it was hopeless looking for her mother in all the chaos, and ducked underneath the refreshment table.

The heavy cloth was still on the table, held there by the weight of the coffee urn and some china bowls. And there, sheltered and unseen, Penny sat nibbling her eclair, still giggling to herself over the Mayor's woes, listening to the cries and crashes and the whooping of the wind all around her. While hoping that something hard and painful would be blown down on to the robbers.

It was as if thinking about them somehow brought them. Over the noise of the devastation she suddenly heard the voices of the robbers, right beside the table where she was hiding. She could even see their feet, on the other side of the table-cloth. And she forgot about the eclair and every-thing as she listened, trembling, to their terrifying words.

"You see where she went?" Ed was asking in his sharp voice. "She just disappeared somewhere. Weird."

"It's *all* weird," Frank said uneasily. "Like this wind. An' how the girl got into the cave, if she did. An' her not goin' to the cops . . ."

"Don't let it get to you," Ed told him. "She prob'ly didn't turn us in because she an' whoever helped her have the idea of keepin' the diamonds for themselves. Anyway, she's a *girl*, isn't she? They're the worst. Always doin' weird things."

"So what do we do?" Frank asked.

"We wait," Ed said. "Back in the cave. I still say the girl knows where the diamonds are. So we wait, an' watch the paper for where these Green weirdies are gonna meet next. Then we go, too, an' grab her."

Frank grunted. "It better happen soon. We're runnin' outa food an' money. Runnin' outa *time*, too."

"I know," Ed said grimly. "The girl's really messin' things up for us. So she better tell us about the diamonds when we grab her. Or we'll make her wish she had."

CHAPTER 7

The Protest Goes On

At last the two men moved away from the table. And at last the wind died down, and the people began to recover. When Penny heard her mother's voice calling her name, she was able to break free of her frozen stillness and crawl out from under the table.

Her mother saw her and smiled. "Found a place to hide, did you? I wish I'd joined you . . ." Then her mother looked more closely, and her smile was replaced by a look of concern. "Penny, you're all pale and trembling! Oh, love – were you frightened?"

She wrapped her arms around Penny and Penny hugged her back, desperately. Penny wanted to say that it wasn't the wind that had frightened her but a threat by two dangerous criminals. But the words wouldn't come. She still had no idea how she could explain it all. And she was as unable as ever to tell anyone about the pendant.

In fact, she thought, right *then* would be a very bad time to reveal the pendant's secret. Because what had been a very glossy, expensive room now looked like a war zone. Amid the wreckage of the chandeliers and the scattered and broken chairs, everything – furniture, walls, carpet, people – was daubed and smeared by flying, sticky food, and stained by splashes of coffee. And the people were still stumbling around looking as shaken and dazed as refugees.

Penny was feeling dazed herself, as her mother took her home. She hardly noticed where she was or what was being said, because every bit of her mind was fixed on what the two men had threatened to do. But slowly she began to see that she was in no immediate danger. All she had to do was stay away from any Green meetings, or any place where the robbers might get her. The diamonds could stay in the rabbit-hole, and the robbers could stay waiting in their cave. Forever, as far as she cared.

But then another thought chilled her. What if the robbers got tired of waiting – and came looking for her?

"Mum," she said carefully as they drove along, "you know those two men? Who were in the woods that day?"

"Ed and Frank," her mother said, nodding. "It was so nice of them to turn up, today. But they must have left in a hurry. I wanted to tell them about the Green group's next meeting, but they'd gone."

Penny was relieved to hear it. "Do they have the group's address?" she asked. "Or our address? Or anyone's?"

"I don't think so," her mother said. "Not ours, anyway. Why?"

"Oh," Penny said vaguely, feeling even more relieved, "I was just wondering if ... um ... if they'd be able to find out about meetings ... and things."

Her mother smiled. "It's nice of you to think of them. But don't worry. I'm sure we'll see those two again."

Not if I can help it, Penny thought.

But then they were home, and Penny went upstairs to get washed for supper. She could hear her mother telling the story of the meeting, and the destructive typhoon – along with her father's murmurs of surprise and Alan's hoots of delight. Before she went down, she went into her room and quietly tried to call the one person who could be told the *whole* story of that afternoon, and all the dangers threatening her.

"Glumdole?" she whispered. *"Glumdole!"*

Nothing happened. No cloaked figure appeared out of nowhere. So he is still away, she thought unhappily. Too far away.

Then she heard her own name being called, by her mother. She trotted downstairs in time to watch an extensive report, on the local television news, of the calamitous meeting.

It began in a fairly boring way, reporting the speeches, though the family cheered when Penny's mother asked pointed questions and booed when she was brushed aside by the businessman, Roche. And the camera was still on, pointed in the right direction, when the glass doors suddenly burst open to let in the typhoon.

Everyone jumped when the doors were shattered. And Penny cheered and laughed along with Alan as the calamity unfolded on the screen. The TV people had bravely stuck to their posts so that the camera missed none of the high points – including the Mayor's loss of his wig and being soaked with coffee along with Roche.

At the end, when the newsreader was making a joke about how politicians ought to be used to wind, Alan looked at Penny with envy. "Are you ever *lucky*," he breathed. "I wish *I* could've been there."

Penny's mother pointed out that he *could* have been there if he had taken any interest in the protest. But Penny had stopped listening. She was reliving the moment when she had heard the robbers planning to grab her. And she didn't feel lucky at all.

But if Penny thought she could simply do nothing until all the danger went away, she soon learned otherwise. At breakfast, the very next day.

The Sunday newspaper contained a large story, with pictures, about the strange wind and the disaster at the meeting. Penny's mother, reading some of the story aloud, also read the very last bit of the report.

"The Mayor has announced," her mother read, "that a special launching ceremony will be held on the site in Cheppingstone Woods, on the day when the construction work is to begin. The Mayor will make a keynote speech, and will dig the first shovelful of earth. Special buses will be provided for members of the public who wish to attend."

"Sounds like something to avoid," Penny's father said, "if the Mayor's making another speech. When is it?"

"Next Saturday," her mother said. She slapped the paper down on the table, making Penny jump.

63

"And it's *not* something to avoid. I'll get the Green group organized to be there too. As a . . . a final protest."

"What's the point," asked Penny's father, "if they're starting the construction?"

"It's a principle," her mother said. "To show everyone that the council and this Roche person are ignoring public opinion. To show that we haven't been silenced."

Penny sat very still, not wanting to look at her mother, not wanting to hear what was coming next. But her father was still being doubtful.

"They might not let you have a protest, in the middle of their big ceremony," he said. "The police are sure to be there . . ."

"They can't stop us," Penny's mother said firmly. "As long as it stays peaceful. People have a right to protest. I expect the press and TV will be there, too, so no one will try to shut us up."

She got briskly to her feet, heading for the phone to start organizing things. And Penny, who had been interested in the thought of police being in the woods, was relieved that what she had expected hadn't happened.

But then it did happen.

Alan was grinning at the paper. "Too bad they couldn't have another hurricane or whatever it was,

64

at this ceremony," he said. "I wouldn't mind going, if I could see that."

That brought his mother back into the room. "In fact," she told Alan, "you *are* going. I want this final protest to be as big as possible, so I'll be asking all the Green group to bring their families. Which means that I will certainly be bringing *mine*."

Penny went stiff with fear, while her father and Alan began to offer the usual excuses about all the things they had to do, on Saturday. But their voices faded as they saw the look on Penny's mother's face.

"We're *going*," she said flatly. "*All* of us, as a family. I don't want to hear another word. It's time you all showed some interest in a very important cause." She glanced at Penny with a smile. "At least I can count on you, Penny, to be willing."

She went back to the telephone, and Penny's father glanced wryly around at the children. "I guess we don't have much choice," he said.

"It's not fair," Alan mumbled.

But Penny sat silent, staring at nothing, chilled by the knowledge that it was true, she had no choice. She would have to go.

The question was, she thought, as an icy hollowness began to fill her insides – would she be coming back?

CHAPTER 8

Into the Woods

The cold hollowness was still filling Penny on that next, fateful Saturday as the four of them arrived at the Cheppingstone Woods for the launching ceremony. It had been mostly a silent drive to the woods. Penny's mother had tried to chat a bit, but her father had looked grumpy and just said "Mm" a few times, Alan had sulked and listened to his Walkman and Penny had stared out the window feeling like a condemned prisoner.

Once or twice before the Saturday she had come close to giving in, deciding simply to tell the whole story to her mother or the police or someone. But she didn't – partly out of natural stubbornness, partly because she still hoped that something would turn up, to keep her safe. So nothing much had changed for her. And she was beginning to tremble, as their car turned into the woods. As if for comfort, she put a hand on her front, where the pendant nestled beneath her shirt.

They found that a dirt road had been bulldozed through the woods, towards the site. Penny's mother grew angry at that ugly new gash on the land, while her father grew annoyed at the lack of parking places. There was a clear area at the side of the site, but it was full of official cars and police cars. The public had to find spaces away from the site, among the trees.

So with Penny's parents both in bad tempers and Alan still sulking, no one noticed how pale and shaky Penny looked as they got out of the car

But she began to feel a lot safer when she saw that there was almost no chance of the robbers getting to her on the site. There were plenty of people there, wandering around waiting for the launching ceremony to start. And there was a sizeable squad of uniformed police among them. So, as her fears faded, Penny began to take an interest in what was going on.

She saw that at the centre of the site there was a makeshift platform, with microphones, where no doubt more boring speeches would be made. Near to it, some TV people were preparing their equipment, while other people with tape recorders or notebooks stood around chatting. A few stalls had been set up here and there, selling hot dogs and ice-cream. And some of the people on the site were workmen, not moving too far away from the row of huge yellow earth-moving machines standing silent, looking as if they were waiting to start a race.

Penny ambled away in that direction – and Alan went with her, also drawn to the machines.

"Look at the size of those bulldozers," Alan said, pointing to the two giant machines with heavy metal treads, like tanks, and menacing blades stretching across the front. In the row with them were a few smaller machines that looked like buckets on wheels – for carrying earth, Penny guessed. And also other machines on bigger wheels, with a scraping blade at one end like a mini-bulldozer, but also a large sharp-toothed scoop at the other end, on a long jointed arm. A bit like a fanged mouth on the end of a weirdly angled neck.

"They look sort of like metal dinosaurs," Penny said softly. "Or alien monsters."

Alan nodded, for once not jeering. "I s'pose they do, sort of," he said. "They roar like monsters, too, when they're going. What if they all started up right now and came at us?"

That idea made Penny take a half-step backwards, though the machines remained silent. Then she followed Alan as he wandered away towards the clear area near the machines, where all the official cars were parked.

"There's the Mayor's car," Alan said, pointing. It

was a huge, shiny-black car with some sort of emblem or crest on the side. "And I bet that one belongs to that big businessman, Roche," Alan went on, pointing to an even huger, shinier, white car.

Penny shrugged, not very interested in cars. "We should get back," she said. "Mum will be starting the protest. She wants everybody to hold placards."

Alan sniffed. "Hold yours in front of your face," he muttered. But he went along readily enough as she started back.

They found their mother in the midst of a vigorous argument with a police inspector, which was ending in a draw. The Green group would be allowed to stand at the back of the crowd and to hold up all the placards they wished. But, the inspector said, they would *not* be allowed to shout or make a lot of noise to try to drown the speeches, or to make any other sort of trouble.

Penny's mother pointed out that the Green group had never planned on such activities, then rushed off to supervise the handing out of the placards, which held hopeful messages such as SAVE THE WOODS and FORESTS BEFORE FACTORIES. Finally they all gathered at the back of the good-sized crowd that was waiting, with their hot dogs and ice-creams, for the Mayor to start the launching ceremony.

69

On the platform the Mayor began his speech, sounding just as false and sickly as he had in the town hall, Penny thought. And Roche was next to him looking just as smug and unpleasant. So as the speech droned on Penny stopped listening and stared idly around, feeling restless.

In that moment, out of nowhere, she was struck by what seemed to be an absolutely brilliant idea. About what she could do to solve her problem.

If she had the nerve.

All she had to do, she thought, was sneak away to that grassy slope where the diamonds lay hidden in an old rabbit-hole. If she could get the diamonds, she could then sneak back to the parking area and simply put the diamonds in, or on, one of the police cars. Then, when they were found, the police might search the area and might even catch the robbers. More likely, the robbers would run off – and then, Penny thought, with the diamonds gone the two men would have no more reason to come after her.

She stared over at the parking area where the police cars were standing, along with the Mayor's big black car and Roche's big white one. Trees grew quite thickly up to the edge of that area, so it wouldn't be hard to stay unseen over there.

The hard part would be getting the diamonds – from the slope that lay just above the cave where the robbers were surely hiding.

Even so, she thought, it was a good idea. And for all she knew, the robbers might already have fled from the woods. Or, if they were still there, they'd be staying well hidden inside their cave, taking no chances with all those policemen so close by.

The more she thought about it, the more she was *sure* that right then, that moment, with the police on hand, would be the safest possible time for her to go and get the diamonds.

If she did it very carefully and silently, she told herself, she'd be away with the diamonds without the robbers ever knowing she was there.

She could feel some of the cold hollowness creep back inside her, but she ignored it. Nudging Alan, she handed him her placard and made a silent gesture towards the trees. Then she quietly slipped away, knowing that her brother and everyone would think she was looking for a woodland version of a bathroom. Moments later she was in among the trees, the people and the site lost to view behind her, only the Mayor's voice following, still distantly droning on.

It took her a little while to reach the foot of the slope, next to the over-grown ravine where the robbers' cave was. It took a while because she was moving so slowly, trying not to rustle a single dry leaf or crack a single twig. She grew tense and cold and shaky as she crept on, but at last she got there. Crouching behind a mossy tree-trunk, she peered through the greenery at the thorny thickets in the ravine.

Were they still in the cave? For a moment longer she crouched and stared and wondered, sweating a little despite the cold hollowness inside her. But then she tried to gather her courage. They're either hiding in the cave, she told herself, or they're a long way away. They wouldn't be wandering around in the open. Not today.

She took a deep breath, then straightened up from her crouch. Just creep quietly up the slope, grab the diamonds, and go, she told herself. Nothing to it.

A twig snapped, just behind her.

Before she could turn, rough hands grabbed her – by the shirt, by the arms, one hand clamping over her mouth. And two voices, one sharp and one thick, began laughing an ugly, threatening laughter.

CHAPTER 9

Out of the Trap

"Told you she'd come back," Ed said gleefully, as the two men hoisted Penny up, keeping her mouth covered, and carried her away. "Just like I said. The diamonds *are* hid around here somewhere, an' she's come to get them."

Frank gave another short ugly laugh. "Must've thought we'd be gone," he growled, "with all the cops around."

"Thought wrong, then," Ed snarled, as they pushed their way through the thickets towards the cave.

Penny was nearly fainting with shock and terror, hanging limply in their hands as they carried her along. When they got to the cave, she knew, they would force her to tell them where the diamonds were. *How* they would do that, she didn't want to guess. Nor did she want to think about what would happen to her afterwards.

Instead, she clung to the only thing that was keeping any scrap of courage alive within her. She had the pendant. And, as she saw the cave ahead, with the barrier standing open and the narrow slit in the cliff gaping like a mouth, she threw the pendant's magic against the robbers.

At least, she tried to.

Perhaps she hadn't got it clear in her frightened mind what she wanted the pendant to *do*. Or perhaps the damaged, unreliable magic just let her down once more.

The pendant failed to grow even faintly warm. And nothing at all happened to Ed and Frank.

They simply strode on, carrying her into the cave, where they dropped her roughly on to one of the narrow cots.

She lay still for a moment, dazed, crushed by the pendant's failure. Around her the cave seemed the same as before, in the dimness, with the stream of water gurgling into the pool at the back. A cheerful sound, as if nothing dreadful could possibly happen there.

But something dreadful seemed about to happen, as Ed and Frank dug some nylon cord out of a knapsack and began to tie her up. She tried to struggle, then to fight them, but she wasn't strong enough. They held her down and bound her, pulling the knots tight around her wrists and ankles.

Then the two men loomed over the cot, glaring down at her.

"Right, girlie," Ed rasped. "You're gonna tell us where the diamonds are."

Penny stared up at them, silent, trembling within her bonds. And she flinched as Ed bent over to bring his face close to hers.

"We don't *want* to have to hurt you," he said, showing his teeth in a half-smile. "If you tell us, we'll let you go. Promise."

Penny still said nothing, knowing that the promise was as false as the smile.

"But we can *make* you talk," Frank snarled, "if that's the way you want it."

Penny flinched again, knowing that she had only one chance. The diamonds weren't *that* important to her, she thought. And if the two thugs went off to find the loot, she might be able to get away.

"I put them in a rabbit-hole," she told them, her voice shaky. "Near the top of the slope." She moved her eyes to show where she meant. "Above the cave."

"*Above* us?" Frank said, astonished. "That close, all this time? Cheeky little so-and-so . . ."

"Good girl," Ed said, grinning. "Saved yourself some trouble." He jerked his head at Frank. "Let's

76

go find the hole. Keep her quiet while we're out."

Frank grabbed her again and slapped something sticky across her mouth. Tape, Penny thought – like the heavy tape that had sealed the bag of diamonds. Then the two men left, jamming the barrier back into place across the cave mouth.

Darkness filled the cave, and fear crept through the darkness, trying to grip Penny more tightly than the ropes. But she fought the fear just as she struggled against the ropes, twisting and wriggling on the smelly cot.

Until, in the midst of her struggle, she heard the men's voices again, through the air-hole that led from the ridge down through the cave's ceiling.

"So she was tellin' the truth," she heard Ed say, his sharp voice gloating. "Diamonds are all here. She didn't even open the bag."

"What do we do with her, then?" Frank asked.

Penny went very still in the darkness, eyes wide, as she listened for the answer.

"She can stay as she is," Ed said carelessly. "All those people will come lookin' for her soon enough – cops too, prob'ly. I say we just leave all that junk in the cave, take the diamonds an' get *out* of here, now, fast as we can."

"How do we go *fast*?" Frank growled. "We got a long walk to get anywhere."

"We're not walkin'," Ed told him. "We're gonna sneak over to where those bigwigs left their cars, an' see how easy it is to steal one."

Frank chortled. "Nice one, Ed," he said, his voice starting to fade as they moved away.

For a moment Penny remained still, relief washing over her with the knowledge that they weren't coming back. And with the relief, her fear died away. The robbers thought she'd have to wait for someone to find her in the cave. But, she said to herself, they were wrong.

Please, pendant, she said in her mind. Don't let me down again. Get me out of these ropes.

The pendant obeyed exactly.

Joy filled her as she felt the reassuring warmth under her shirt. But then she was hoisted into the air with a sudden, breathtaking jerk. She had told the pendant to "get her out of the ropes", and it was doing just that.

As the magic's force lifted her, the ropes snapped and fell away like rotten thread. But Penny went on being lifted – and *thrown*, as if she was weightless, head over heels through the air, across the cave.

She landed in a sitting position, with a huge splash, in the midst of the pool made by the stream that poured into the back of the cave.

The shock of the flight and the sudden, icy drenching would have made Penny scream, but for the tape over her mouth. But when she ripped the tape away and stood up in the pool, she felt more like cheering, or laughing, than screaming.

She was free – and unharmed, for the water had given her a painless landing, at the cost of being dripping wet. Now only the barrier across the cave-mouth stood in her way. Staring at it, she felt anger surge up inside her at the memory of what the robbers had intended for her. I'll fix *them*, she thought.

She aimed the pendant's power at the barrier. And some of her anger may have found its way into the magic. The pendant did not merely open the barrier, as it had before. The magic took hold of the barrier and destroyed it.

It was like an immense crushing force, coming down on to the heavy planks and corrugated iron as if a vast invisible foot was stamping on it. The planks snapped and splintered into kindling. The sheets of metal were crumpled and compacted, the way someone might wad up sheets of paper into a ball. Open-mouthed, Penny watched in silence as the pendant showed just how powerful its magic could be.

But right then, she thought, it could be as

powerful as it liked. As long as the robbers didn't get away.

She ran out past the wreckage of the barrier, plunged through the thickets of the ravine, then sped away through the woods as fast as the tangle of branches would allow. Soon she arrived at the edge of the construction site – and stopped, amazed. Everything was almost the same, for in reality only a few minutes had passed since she had slipped away from the protest.

The crowd was still standing where it had been, with the knot of Green protestors still holding up their placards. The Mayor and Roche and the other bigwigs had come down from the platform, and the Mayor – holding the shiniest spade Penny had ever seen – was self-importantly getting ready to dig the first shovelful of earth, as the ceremonial start to the construction. Roche and the other officials were also looking pleased with themselves, while the photographers and TV people clustered around. Every eye on the site was fixed on the Mayor's smug smile and the spade he was holding. Even the police had moved close to the group and were watching carefully.

No one was looking anywhere else. No one saw the two men in leather jackets creep out from the trees by the parking area. No one saw them creep up to the big white car, which surely belonged to Roche, and with shocking ease get a door open. No one saw the small puff of exhaust smoke as the car started, no one heard the rich quiet purr of the car's engine.

No one but Penny.

She began to run forward from the edge of the site, as the white car also started to move. She called out, but she was still too far away. Only one or two people turned, frowning a little at what they thought was just a noisy child.

The white car picked up speed, rolling quietly past the silent row of huge yellow earth-moving machines.

Penny gave up trying to call to the people. It was too late, anyway. None of them, not even the police, could hope to stop the robbers. It was up to her.

Stop that car, she said to the pendant – urgently, anxiously, and still with much of the anger that she had felt before, in the cave.

As in the cave, the pendant obeyed. As best it could. And at full power.

One of the enormous bulldozers, in that row of silent machines, came roaring into life.

Penny was startled, having expected the pendant to do something to the stolen white car itself. She peered intently at the bulldozer, but there was definitely no driver in its cab. Many of the work-men, and some of the people in the crowd around the Mayor, also turned to stare at the bulldozer, looking startled.

They looked even more amazed to see Roche's big white car being driven away.

And then everyone – including Penny – became transfixed with shock as the bulldozer, still clearly without a driver, bellowed as if in rage and lunged forward. Into the path of the white car.

CHAPTER 10

Monster Machines

The robbers saw the bulldozer only at the last minute. They tried to avoid it, steering sharply away, tyres skidding a little. But it was too late.

The bulldozer's giant blade struck the side of the car with a crunching clang. The car had no chance against that power. It was forced sideways, wheels spinning helplessly. Then the bulldozer blade heaved up – and flipped the car, with more metallic crunching, on to its back.

The robbers, dazed and stunned, had no chance to get out of the crumpled car. The bulldozer backed up, still bellowing monstrously, and with its blade scraped up a heap of soil against one side of the car. Then – with startling speed – it wheeled around to the other side, and shoved another bladeful of earth against the car. The earth held the car doors firmly shut. The robbers were trapped.

By then a number of people, including the

workmen and the police, were running towards the car. But they halted, for the bulldozer swung towards them, lifting its blade high as if threateningly.

And that was when things, and machines, got completely out of hand.

All the other machines in that row started their engines.

To Penny, staring, it was as if every machine had come to life – having been given a kind of life, and a mind of its own, by the pendant.

The trouble was that the "minds" of the machines seemed insane.

Several of the big digging machines, with their scoops on the ends of long arms, began rolling around in crazy circles, scooping up huge gobbets of dirt and flinging them in all directions.

The earth-carrying machines, the ones like great buckets on wheels, careened away at high speed, zig-zagging across the site, scattering the people, bumping into each other, crashing into the make-shift platform and leaving it in splinters.

And the second giant bulldozer set off, snorting and bellowing, directly towards all the cars parked in the official parking space.

When the second bulldozer reached the cars, it did not pause or even slow down. Its monstrous

treads rolled unstoppably on – over the big black shiny car that was the Mayor's. It treated the car just like a bump on the ground, grinding up on to it, with metal and glass shrieking and crunching, then rolling on to leave the big car looking like a tin can that had been stamped flat.

On the edge of the site, Penny watched with growing horror. All over the open area people were yelling and screaming and running, trying to dodge the crazed earth-carriers, trying to protect themselves from the heavy showers of dirt flung by the diggers. Penny saw that the Mayor had lost his wig again, and that he and Roche were covered in muddy clay as they scrambled around with the others, looking for safety.

But there was nothing to smile at, this time. This was not a high wind blowing bits of food around. This was deadly danger.

"Stop it," Penny whispered.

But she felt no answering warmth from the pendant, and around her nothing changed. The machines still roared on with their crazed antics. By then Roche's white car had been almost totally buried by the first bulldozer, while the second one had rumbled on to flatten the television van and was heading for a police car. The wheeled diggers, still scooping and hurling huge chunks of earth, were steadily moving towards the terrified groups of people who were trying to hide among the trees at the edge of the site. And the berserk buckets-on-wheels were still rushing wildly around, keeping the people penned where they were.

As Penny watched, one of the earth-carriers and one of the diggers came together – and charged crazily towards a knot of people sheltering among some spindly fir trees.

A knot of people carrying placards. The Green group – including Penny's family.

"Stop it!" Penny yelled. But she could barely hear herself in the monstrous noise from the site, the bellowing machines, the cries of terrified people, the crunch and crackle of trees and boards and cars being flattened and destroyed.

The pendant also seemed not to hear. At least, it failed again to obey. Its metal stayed cool, and the machines went right on with their insane destructions, their deadly charge.

"Stop the machines!" Penny shrieked. "Get them *away*, stop them, *stop them!*"

The pendant went fiercely hot against her skin.

Her first order, just to "stop it", may have been too vague to call on the magic. Telling it to stop the *machines* was more effective. Especially when the order contained all Penny's horror at the damage and fear for her family.

Every one of the machines came to a sudden halt, including the two that were charging at the Green group. The first bulldozer stopped burying the white car, now entirely out of sight. The second bulldozer came to a stop while sitting on the remains of a police car. The diggers dropped their scoopsful of earth, the earth-carriers halted their mad zig-zagging.

But though they stopped, they did not shut off. Their engines went on running, the roars softening to a low muttering.

And all the machines stood still, looking and sounding as if they were somehow poised and ready for something. As if they were *waiting*.

There was near-silence on the site in that moment, save for the throbbing rumble of the machines, and some moans and whimpers from the frightened people. Then several voices were raised in different shouts. The police inspector, barking orders to his men. A foreman, organizing the workmen to do something about the machines. Many other people, including the Mayor, babbling aloud with shock and disbelief and anger and relief.

And among them rose the voice of Penny's mother in a piercing cry of anxiety, the cry of a mother whose child is missing in the midst of disaster.

"PEN-NY!"

"Here!" Penny yelled, at the top of her voice.

It was probably the worst thing she could have said. The pendant had more or less obeyed her when she called on it to "stop the machines". But she had also said "get them away". If the machines seemed to be waiting, it may have been because the pendant was also waiting – to be told *where* it should send the machines that its wild magic had brought to life.

Penny's one-word cry, to her mother, seemed to be what the pendant and all the machines were waiting for.

But of course the pendant's response was as way-ward and unpredictable as ever.

All the huge engines roared and bellowed once again. All the machines turned, like a monstrous army of yellow metal, and charged.

At Penny.

CHAPTER 11

Running for her Life

By then Penny had already started trotting out on
to the site, while the people were starting to come
out of hiding. As the machines began their charge,
the people howled and fled again. And Penny
stopped, not sure what was happening.

Then she realized that the charge was aimed at
her. The machines were slowly forming up in an
orderly way as they thundered towards her. The
two mighty bulldozers, slower than the others,
were at the centre, grinding steadily forward. On
either side were the wheeled diggers, scoops held
high like weapons, moving much faster. And at
each end of the massed rank, the earth-carriers were
taking their places, hurtling forward as the fastest
of all.

Penny took a step back, staring, hardly able to
believe that it could be happening. Then she whirled and dashed away to her left, thinking that she
could get out of the path of the charge. But some

earth-carriers roared forward even faster, cutting her off, driving her back. Back into the path of the advancing machines.

The familiar iciness of fear filled her once again. She turned and fled, running for her life. Back the way she had come. Back towards the cave.

As she sprinted away through the woods, she glanced fearfully back. The machines were still bellowing along after her, and the speedier ones seemed to have gained on her a little. And then she learned that it is not a good idea to look backwards when you are running through woods. With a crash and a shriek, she ran headlong into a bush.

The branches clutched at her, as if trying to hold her hostage for the machines. Icy terror clutched at her as well as she fought her way clear. The machines had gained on her even more, and the swift earth-carriers were rushing farther forward at either side of the charge – as if trying to get past and around her, to cut off her escape.

She dodged around the bush and ran on. But panic was draining her strength while the thick brush and uneven ground were slowing her up. The machines, on the other hand, crashed through and over the woods as if no barriers existed – steering around the larger trees but otherwise flattening everything in their path.

And they were still gaining on Penny. And

gained more when a root tripped her so that she fell in a heap. She scrambled up, sobbing, gasping for breath, and ran on in a wavering half-stumble.

Please, pendant, she begged silently as she ran. Stop them. Stop the machines. Now. Please.

But again the unreliable magic chose that moment to fail entirely. The pendant remained cool on her chest. And the unequal race went on. One small terrified girl, blood on her face from lashing twigs mingling with tears of desperation and panic, pursued by that giant army of maddened yellow metal.

No one was there to help her. Her parents and the police and all the people were far behind, out of sight. She cried out the name of Glumdole, in a despairing shriek, but nothing happened. Her magical friend was still away, out of reach. No one was coming to save her.

She staggered on through the tangled brush. The thunder of giant engines was like a wall of sound behind her. She could feel the heat of those engines, like the hot breath of hunting animals closing in on their prey. At any second she expected to feel the bite of a scoop's huge teeth or the crushing impact of a bulldozer's blade.

Ahead, she saw the grassy slope of the ridge that marked the edge of the basin where the construction site lay. The ridge above the robbers' cave, where she had hidden the diamonds – which seemed to have been months rather than days before.

A flicker of hope lent her a small burst of speed. The steep slope, she thought, might slow the machines down. She might be able to dash over the ridge, down the far side, and around into the ravine in front of the cave. If the machines pursued her into the narrow ravine, they might get tangled up, blocking each other's path. And she might be safe from them in the cave . . .

Those thoughts, those desperate plans, flashed through her mind in instants as she fled towards the ridge. Up the grassy slope she dashed, as fast as her aching legs would go. Near the top of the slope she risked a glance back, and saw that the machines had slowed a little, that she had gained on them a little. Her idea looked like it might work . . .

And then she stopped, on the ridge-top, and screamed.

Some of the fast-moving earth-carriers had got well ahead of the main army of machines. They had already crossed over the ridge, farther along from where Penny stood.

They were on the far side of the ridge, roaring towards her, barring her path.

And behind her, giant scoops reaching out like clutching hands, the diggers were thundering up the slope, with the mighty bulldozers behind them.

She was surrounded.

She screamed again, in terror and despair. "Pendant!" she cried. "*Stop the machines!*"

Still there was no response from the cold lump of metal under her shirt.

And the machines drew closer.

"*Help* me!" she screamed, in her panic. "*Lift me up!*"

Once before she had asked the pendant to lift her into the air, out of danger, but she had merely been put into greater danger.

This time, the pendant managed merely to *leave* her in danger.

The metal grew warm against her chest, but only slightly. And the pendant lifted her up – but only about two feet above the ground.

While right in front of her, one of the diggers was swinging its fearsome scoop down as if aiming to chop her in half.

As she screamed again, the pendant's magic gave an uneven little jerk, hoisting her another foot or so from the ground.

The digger missed her by the width of her smallest finger.

94

Instead, the heavy toothed scoop bit deep into the soft ground at the top of the ridge. As it stuck there, it brought the digger itself to an abrupt halt, almost toppling it over. Another digger crashed into the back of it, and other machines collided wildly with them in a sudden pile-up.

On the other side of the ridge, the leading earth-carrier had also almost reached the top when its front wheel hit a large rabbit-hole. The jolt threw the machine sharply sideways, rolling it crunchingly on to its side. The other carriers, charging up behind it, crashed into it – their charge also halted in another crushing, grinding pile-up.

Suddenly both sides of the ridge were in total chaos – an immense tangled shambles of yellow machinery and the monstrous noise of tortured metal and howling, over-strained engines.

But something else as well was being over-strained.

The pile-ups of machines were of course on the ridge that was the roof of the robbers' cave. And the stone and earth of that roof, with its old and rotting supports, had never had to put up with such an immense weight, nor with such ferocious gouging blows from diggers' scoops and bull-dozers' blades.

With a gigantic crash, like the mightiest of earth-

95

quakes, the entire roof of the cave – that whole section of the ridge – collapsed, in a blinding and deafening eruption of dirt and dust.

CHAPTER 12

And Then a Fountain

"Goodness me," Glumdole said, blinking mournfully. "Where were you then?"

"Still in mid-air," Penny said. "In the middle of this huge cloud of dust, with the ground a lot farther away, below me." She shook her head, remembering. "So I told the pendant to put me down..."

Glumdole was shaking his head too. "Oh, Pen*e*lope," he said. "It might have put you *any*where."

"I know," she said quickly. "But luckily it put me down very, very slowly. As if the pendant was tired or something. On the way down I got a look at the woods, beyond the ridge, where the machines had cut this huge sort of path through the trees. All the people were running along it – coming to my rescue, I suppose. But they couldn't see me through all the dust."

"Just as well," Glumdole murmured.

"So I was put down," Penny went on. "On top of all the dirt that had fallen into the cave. Right next to all the machines that had fallen in, too. And some of them were still working – the ones that weren't upside down or smashed. They were still *digging*, Glumdole, with their scoops and blades, like wild crazy things, down there at the bottom of that huge hole."

"But you were safe?" Glumdole asked.

"Oh, yes," she assured him. "I started climbing out, and the people got to the edge of the hole looking really amazed to see me ... and my mum was crying ... and some men started down to get me. And then it happened."

But she had to pause there, because the memory started to make her laugh. And Glumdole watched her in gloomy silence as she went off in a gale of giggles.

Glumdole had come to Penny's room the very next day after what a newspaper had called the Cheppingstone Calamity. Penny's mother had insisted that she rest after the terrors of the day before – so she had been lying on her bed listening to music and feeling bored when Glumdole appeared out of nothing to say that he was back. And when he had heard a bit about her adventures,

Glumdole suggested they go to his house where she could tell him the rest of the story over tea.

His home was underground – under some hills not too far from Cheppingstone Woods. It had no windows, but otherwise it was cosy and charming with lots of warm rugs and bright pictures and soft, cushiony chairs. It was also very clean, as a home would be when the owner can do housework by magic. Tea and cakes and biscuits appeared the same way, and Penny curled up in a low armchair to eat and to tell Glumdole all about the disaster in the woods. Except when she was interrupted by fits of giggles, as she was just then, recalling how the disaster had come to an end.

"It was the stream, of course," she said at last. "The one that ran through the cave and then went underground."

It seemed that all the crazy, aimless digging that the half-ruined machines went on doing, down in the collapsed cave, broke through to the stream. So as all the people crowded around the edge of the huge hole, staring down at the wreckage and at Penny, the stream burst out like a fountain and drenched everyone with cold muddy water.

By some chance, the Mayor and Mr Roche were standing closest to where the water burst out, and they got the worst soaking. But everyone else got wet while they lifted Penny up out of the hole and away, back to the half-ruined construction site.

And as they went, the water followed them.

Back on the site, Penny saw that Mr Roche's car had been dug out of the dirt, and the robbers dug out of the car. They were in handcuffs, looking miserable, and the police inspector was holding the bag of diamonds, looking pleased.

But then the water arrived.

The underground stream had become an over-ground stream, flowing from the ridge. And every-one was soon reminded that the construction site was in a huge natural *basin* – because the flow of water was starting to fill it.

So everyone left, quickly. And because the official cars had been mostly wrecked by the crazed bull-dozers, everyone had to beg rides with the ordinary folk – whose cars had been farther away, and were safe.

"The TV people came back in our car," Penny told Glumdole happily. "They *interviewed* me, too. Asking about what happened when all the machines were chasing me." She giggled again. "If they only knew *why* . . ."

"What did you say?" Glumdole asked doubtfully.

"I just said I'd been too scared to know what was happening, really. I said I just ran, and then the ground collapsed."

"Hmm," Glumdole said. "And they believed you?"

"Course. They didn't know any better. No one had *any* idea what happened, or how." Penny grinned. "I was on TV last night!"

Glumdole sighed gloomily. "Let's hope it's all quickly forgotten, Penelope. Once people have found some sort of explanation that they can believe."

"What if people guess that it was magic?" Penny asked.

"It's unlikely," Glumdole said. "Humans will go to any lengths, will dream up the silliest ideas and theories, to explain strange happenings. But, nowadays, they'll *never* think it might be magic. Still, you would be wise not to use the pendant again for a while. In fact, Penelope, now that it has put you into danger again, don't you think it should be destroyed? Before something worse happens?"

Penny frowned. "I don't know, Glumdole. It seems . . . unfair. It's not the pendant's fault that its magic was damaged." She looked up brightly at her friend. "But I *will* put it away again. And I promise not to use it – unless I really, really have to."

"Very well," Glumdole said, sighing. "And now, I suppose I should send you home. Before someone looks into your room to see how you are."

Penny nodded. "Thank you for tea, Glumdole. I'm glad you're back."

"I'll visit you again soon, Penelope," he said. "Remember to put the pendant away."

Then he raised a long finger, twitched the pointed tip of one ear, and Penny was back in her room.

Just in time, too, for her father was tapping on her door – then opening it to tell her that local TV was doing another programme, right then, on what had happened at Cheppingstone Woods.

"We can watch our own TV star again," he said with a smile.

Downstairs, Penny settled beside her mother as the programme began. It was a little boring at first, re-telling the whole story – about the plan to build factories in the woods, and the Green group's protests. There were some clips of the first disaster with the typhoon in the town hall, including another glimpse of Penny's mother that made her father say there were *two* TV stars in the family.

Then the programme got on to the launching ceremony, in the woods, and how it ended in disaster. Finally it showed Penny emerging from the huge hole where the cave had fallen in, and the fountain of water that burst out to flood the site. The camera lingered for a moment on a picture of Alan, soaked and muddy and furious – "looking like a drowned gerbil", Penny said teasingly.

That made Alan furious all over again, but his parents silenced him so they could watch the repeated bits of the interview with Penny. Then, best of all, the programme reported some new details.

First, the two robbers were in jail, facing long prison sentences. "They seemed so *nice*," Penny's mother murmured, making Penny look at her oddly.

Then, the best news of all. Cheppingstone Woods was to be saved.

The TV showed the huge basin where the construction site was to have been. A great deal of it was now a small lake, hiding most of the scars caused by the machines. And Mr Roche told the TV reporter, angrily, that he was selling the land back to the council and would build his factories on a disused railway yard on the edge of town.

"Where they should have been in the first place," Penny's mother said with satisfaction.

Then the Mayor, still looking a bit dazed, came on the TV to say that the woods – with the new lake in their midst – would go back to being a protected area, a place of recreation for the towns-people. And a brand-new glint appeared in the eyes of Penny's mother.

"I know," she said. "The Green group can start a new campaign. To make that lake a sanctuary for wild birds."

"For wild bulldozers, more like," Alan muttered.

Meanwhile the TV reporter had brought on a scientist with large glasses who began earnestly trying to explain why so many machines should all go crazy in the same place at the same time.

Penny didn't understand much of it. But the idea seemed to be that it was some combination, all at once, of sunspots, "electromagnetic fields", some stray radiation and perhaps small earth tremors.

As the TV reporter nodded wisely, clearly understanding no more of it than Penny, her father snorted.

"What nonsense!" he scoffed. "Just a lot of words that mean nothing. The man hasn't got a *clue* how it happened. No one has. Scientists are *baffled*, the paper said." He chuckled. "The next thing will be, someone will come on TV and say it all happened by *magic*."

And he laughed loudly at his joke, and Penny's mother and Alan laughed along with him. And no one noticed that Penny was simply smiling a little smile, all to herself.

Alex Martin
Boris the Tomato £2.99

Boris is big, intelligent and one of the most popular vegetables in Mr Lymer's greenhouse. But this is not enough. Boris wants power. He wants total tomato supremacy – in and *outside* the greenhouse.

Soon Boris and his tomato troops are squeezing the life out of all the other plants. Will Boris rule the day? Or has he got too big for his skin . . .?

Joke van Leeuwen
The Story of Bobble who Wanted to be Rich £2.99

Ever ridden in a tricycle-van or slept in a hammock? Ever kept a bat for a pet? Bobble has . . . but then Bobble is 'different', and so are her parents. The trouble is, they haven't much money.

So one night, Bobble decides to become rich. A letter to Uncle Fogey should do it. Only his ideas aren't *quite* what Bobble had in mind . . .

'Rich and enigmatic . . . full of laughter, irony and longing.'
BOOKS FOR YOUR CHILDREN

Saviour Pirotta
Supper with the Spooks £2.99

The ghost turned huge, sad eyes on him. 'I have used most of my energy to wander so far from my burial place,' he said. 'I beg you, this time to hear me out.'

A daring burglar is plotting to steal Mongley, an ancient sword, from Arundel Castle. Mongley belongs to a giant called Bevis. The trouble is Giant Bevis is . . . a ghost and is powerless to save the sword – and himself.

The only people who can stop the robbery are two local schoolchildren: Alec and Indira. Will their plan work? If they fail, what will happen to the swordless ghost? Will he be doomed to haunt the castle for ever?

All Pan books are available at your local bookshop or newsagent, or can be ordered direct from the publisher. Indicate the number of copies required and fill in the form below.

Send to: Pan C. S. Dept
                Macmillan Distribution Ltd
                Houndmills Basingstoke RG21 2XS
or phone: 0256 29242, quoting title, author and Credit Card number.

Please enclose a remittance* to the value of the cover price plus: £1.00 for the first book plus 50p per copy for each additional book ordered.

*Payment may be made in sterling by UK personal cheque, postal order, sterling draft or international money order, made payable to Pan Books Ltd.

Alternatively by Barclaycard/Access/Amex/Diners

Card No.

Expiry Date

Signature:

Applicable only in the UK and BFPO addresses

While every effort is made to keep prices low, it is sometimes necessary to increase prices at short notice. Pan Books reserve the right to show on covers and charge new retail prices which may differ from those advertised in the text or elsewhere.

NAME AND ADDRESS IN BLOCK LETTERS PLEASE:

....

Name _____

Address _____

_____

_____

_____

6/92